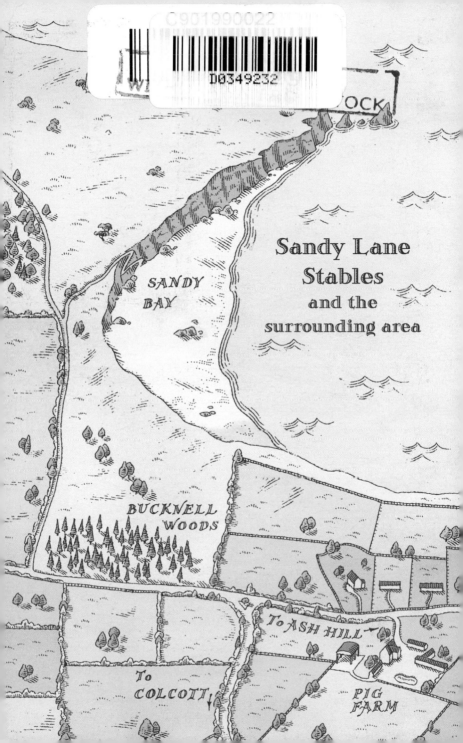

Sandy Lane
Stables
and the
surrounding area

SANDY
BAY

BUCKNELL
WOODS

To ASH HILL

To
COLCOTT

PIG
FARM

Sandy Lane Stables

Sandy Lane Stables

Strangers at the Stables

Michelle Bates

Adapted by: Caroline Young

Reading consultant: Alison Kelly

Series editor: Lesley Sims

Designed by: Brenda Cole

Cover and inside illustrations: Barbara Bongini and Ian McNee

Map illustrations: John Woodcock

This edition first published in 2016 by Usborne Publishing Ltd.,
Usborne House, 83-85 Saffron Hill, London EC1N 8RT, England.
www.usborne.com

Copyright © Usborne Publishing 2016, 2009, 2003, 1997

Illustrations copyright © Usborne Publishing, 2016

The name Usborne and the devices ♀ ⊕ are Trade Marks of
Usborne Publishing Ltd. UKE

A CIP catalogue record for this book is available from the British Library.

Contents

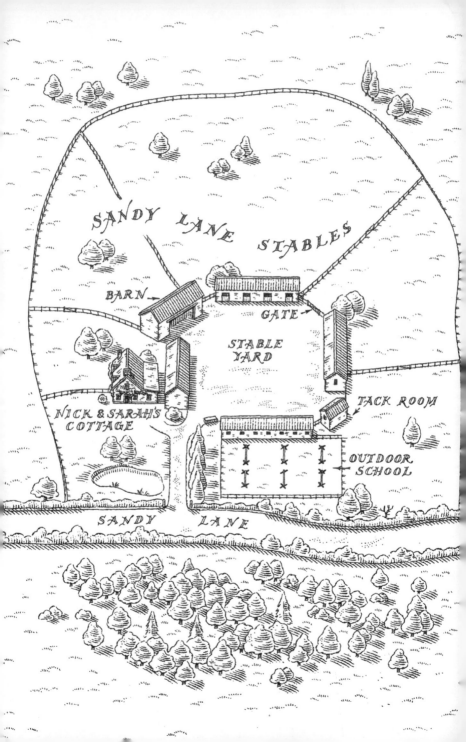

Chapter 1

Some Bad News

"If we have to close down the stables, we'll close down the stables."

Rosie Edwards froze. She was standing outside the tack room at Sandy Lane stables, and had just heard the owner, Nick Brooks, talking on the phone. She really wished she hadn't. Surely Nick and his wife Sarah weren't thinking of closing the stables? Everything was going so well... It just didn't make any sense.

Rosie simply couldn't imagine life without Sandy Lane. It had been hard for all of her family, uprooting themselves with her father's job, but hardest of all for Rosie – new home, new school, new friends. It wasn't until she'd discovered Sandy Lane that she started to feel settled again. Here at the stables she'd made all of her friends, including her best friend, Jess Adams. Rosie felt hot tears pricking her eyes as she remembered how awful it had been before she had known any of them.

"Right, we'll have to discuss it with Beth immediately," Rosie heard Sarah saying. Rosie strained her ears, but she couldn't catch Nick's reply. Then, before she had even had time to step out of the way, the door of the tack room flung open and Nick strode out. Rosie jumped back, embarrassed.

"I didn't see you there. Are you okay, Rosie?" Nick said, breathlessly.

"Yes, fine Nick." Rosie swallowed hard. "I was just... er... wondering. What time do you want us in the outdoor school?"

"Well let me see – " Nick was cut short when his mobile phone rang. Smiling apologetically at Rosie, he hurried towards the cottage to take the call.

Rosie sighed. She had no idea what to make of it all. Crossing the yard, she saw Kate and Alex Hardy, two of the Sandy Lane regulars, sprinting up the drive, late as usual. By the gate, Tom Buchanan, Sandy Lane's star rider, sprang neatly into the saddle of his horse, Chancey. It was the start of the Easter holidays, and everyone was in high spirits.

"All ready for the Tentenden training this morning?" came a voice from behind her. Rosie spun round to see her friend Jess, smiling widely as she hopped off her bike.

"Sort of," Rosie answered flatly. It was their first training session for this year's Tentenden Team Chase, and normally any mention of the cross-country race made Rosie shiver with excitement. The day Nick had announced that she, Tom, Charlie and Jess would make up the cross-country team had been one of the best days of her life. But this morning's phone call had taken away all her enthusiasm – what was the point, if the stables were closing?

Jess sensed something was up immediately. "Are you okay, Rosie?"

"Well, can I tell you something?" Rosie whispered. Jess was Rosie's best friend, and Rosie knew she could tell her anything. "It's something awful..."

"What is it, Rosie?" Jess frowned.

Taking a deep breath, Rosie blurted out everything about the phone call and the possibility of the stables closing down. "What do you think it can mean, Jess?" Rosie finished. "It sounds as though they're going to pack it all in."

"Nick and Sarah would never leave Sandy Lane – not without telling us, anyway," Jess said, firmly. "Are you sure you heard things right?"

"Of course I did," Rosie insisted.

"There's Charlie. Let's ask if he knows anything about it." Jess waved across the yard. "Charlie!"

Charlie Marshall looked up from where he was sweeping the yard. "What's up?" he asked, ambling over to speak to them.

As Rosie repeated her story about the phone call, Charlie listened carefully.

"Hmm... Doesn't sound like anything to worry about to me," Charlie said when Rosie had finished.

"Tell her it's nonsense," Jess begged, "or we'll never hear the end of it."

"Why doesn't anyone ever believe me?" Rosie snapped, feeling hurt.

"It's not that we don't believe you, Rosie. It's just that it seems so unlikely." Charlie shrugged. "Sandy Lane's had its rough patches, but it's come through all that. And Nick and Sarah would hardly have taken Beth on as the new stable girl if they were about to close down, would they? There will be some explanation, you'll see."

Rosie looked unconvinced. "But I don't think this is something they expected, Charlie. It sounded like something out of the blue."

"Well, there's no point panicking. Nick will tell us everything in good time." Charlie looked at his watch. "Right, I'm going to tack up Napoleon."

"We'd better get a move on as well, if we're going to get our horses ready," Jess said.

"Hang on, here's Nick right now." Charlie waved at Nick, who was striding across the yard. "Let's ask him what's going on."

"No... no, don't do that," Rosie said urgently. "It'll look as though I was listening in on them."

"Well, you were," Charlie said, grinning.

Rosie shot him a dirty look. "I know, but I don't want Nick to know that."

"Folks, I'll be taking the training session at eleven," Nick called out across the yard. "Then I need to see everybody in the tack room at twelve. Can you lot spread the word? I've got some important news for you all. And if you see Beth, can you tell her to come and find me at the cottage?"

"Told you so," Rosie said, as Nick hurried off. Jess and Charlie looked worried now, too.

"Hmm, I think we ought to tell the others what Rosie heard," said Jess. "Just so that everyone knows, and can prepare themselves."

Charlie nodded. "I suppose you're right."

Rosie went into Pepper's stable, and began to give his black and white coat a quick going over with the body brush. "Whatever are we going to do, Pepper?" she murmured.

"Talking to yourself, Rosie?" Beth's smiling face appeared at the door of Pepper's stable.

"There you are, Beth." Rosie looked up. "Nick's looking for you. He wants you to meet him at the cottage with Sarah."

"Sounds serious. Hope I'm not about to get the sack!" Beth laughed.

Rosie tried to smile back, but it wasn't easy. Beth was the new stable girl. She hadn't been at Sandy Lane long, but she'd fitted in straight away. Everybody liked and respected her, and she was absolutely brilliant with the horses.

After she'd finished with the body brush, Rosie went to collect Pepper's saddle from the tack room. Word must have spread about the phone call – everyone was looking gloomy. Sighing, Rosie hurried back to Pepper's stable and tacked him up, before leading him over to join the others. Tom, Charlie and Jess were already making their way down to the outdoor school.

"All here?" Nick called, opening the gate. "I want everyone to start by mounting and dismounting properly on both sides. Then start walking around. I'll let you know when I want you to trot on. I'd like to see some turns on the forehand from a halt, rising trot on each diagonal and cantering on a named leg. Tom, you take the lead."

Tom led the way around the perimeter and Rosie brought up the rear. She tried to concentrate, but Pepper was restless and fidgeting. Charlie couldn't get Napoleon to respond either, and Storm Cloud was refusing to trot forwards for Jess.

"Come on everyone," Nick said, irritably. "Pay attention, please."

"One two, one two, one two," Rosie chanted, trying desperately to stop Pepper from trotting into the back of Chancey.

After twenty minutes of loosening up their horses, Nick was not impressed. "I think everyone's made enough of a mess of those exercises. Let's try some jumping now."

Rosie looked at the course laid out in front of them. The jumps weren't that high, but she suddenly felt nervous.

"Charlie, do you want to start and show us how it's done?" Nick suggested.

"Sure," said Charlie, and with a flourish of his whip, he turned Napoleon to the first.

Rosie held her breath. They were going very fast as they flew over the brush and cantered on to the stile. They soared over the next two fences in swift succession, but Charlie wasn't going to jump clear. As he turned Napoleon to the gate, the little bay refused, and although Charlie turned him three times, he still couldn't get him to jump it.

"Try him over the parallel bars to relax him," Nick called. This worked, and Napoleon cleared them with ease.

Rosie watched grimly as Tom took a turn at the course and knocked down two jumps. And Jess did no better, knocking down three.

"My turn," Rosie muttered, as Nick called her forward. She gritted her teeth and kicked Pepper on for the brush. She jumped clear, but she knew it hadn't been a very impressive round. Not good enough for the team, certainly.

"Right, that's enough for one day," Nick said at the end of the session. "I don't know what's wrong with you lot. You'll have to work a lot harder than that to be ready for Tentenden. It's only four weeks away, you know." He turned to leave, adding, "And don't forget – meeting in the tack room in five."

Gloomily, Rosie led the way back to the yard, taking Pepper to his stable. She was furious with herself. She hated riding badly in front of Nick.

She fumbled with Pepper's girth as she tried to undo the buckle. "I'll be back later to sponge you down," she said, guiltily. She knew she should do it immediately, but the news in the tack room simply couldn't wait.

Slinging Pepper's saddle across her arm, she hurried into the tack room and hung it up on its peg before sitting down.

Nick was leaning against the desk, his arms folded in front of him. He looked deadly serious. "I'll come straight to the point," he said. "I'm afraid Sarah and I have had some rather bad news."

Rosie's heart skipped a beat. This was it: he was going to tell them it was all over for Sandy Lane.

Nick glanced at his wife, Sarah, who sat beside him, and took a deep breath. "Sarah's dad in America has been taken ill. He's had a heart attack and been rushed into hospital."

The room was full of sympathetic mutterings.

"He's going to be all right," Nick went on. "But the doctors say he's going to be in hospital for a while, so we've agreed to go and run his stud farm for him in Kentucky."

Rosie felt a wave of relief flood through her, followed almost immediately by a wave of guilt.

How could she be so selfish? Sarah's father was ill, and all she could think about was the future of her beloved stables.

"We've asked Beth to take charge of Sandy Lane while we're away," Sarah began. "We may be gone for three weeks, but we'll get back sooner if we can. Beth's going to come and live at the cottage until we get back. Nick and I are hoping you lot will be able to help her, especially as it's the Easter holidays. We'd feel a lot happier knowing you were giving Beth a hand."

"Of course we'll help out." Tom nodded. "When are you going?"

"Well..." Nick sighed heavily. "I've managed to get flights for Monday morning, which doesn't give us long to get everything sorted – just two days."

"You'll have to bear with us," Sarah said. Rosie noticed how pale and tired Sarah looked. "There's such a lot to do," she went on. "It's going to be a tough few days for all of us, I think."

"We should be back in time for the Tentenden

Team Chase, but Beth has agreed to continue with the training." Nick glanced around the room. "I'll set up a programme with her before I go. I'm sure everything will be fine, and you can always call us. I'll leave you the mobile number I'll be using while we're away, as well as the contact number of a friend of mine in case of emergency." Nick smiled anxiously. "I'm sure you won't need them. You should be fine with Beth in charge."

As everyone trooped out of the tack room, Rosie realised that the terrible tension in her stomach had gone. Sandy Lane was not closing down after all – thank goodness for that!

Chapter 2

They're Off!

Sarah was right: the next few days were very tough. She and Nick had to draw up rotas for mucking-out, feeding and grooming. They had to sort out lessons and hacks, and establish routines to keep the stables running smoothly. After much discussion, they decided that the regulars were responsible for two horses each and, while Beth would take all private lessons, the regulars would lead hacks.

Eventually, Monday morning arrived and it was time for Nick and Sarah to go.

"I've pinned our contact number on the tack room notice board," Nick called out of the taxi window. "We'll try to get in touch when we get there, but don't panic if you don't hear much from us – we're probably going to have our hands full!"

"We'll be fine," Beth said with a smile. "What can go wrong in three weeks?"

"Do lots of practise," Sarah called. "And remember to send off the Tentenden entry form, please! Someone needs to fill it out and put it in the post – the deadline's not far off!"

As the taxi disappeared, Rosie began tacking up Blackjack and Pepper – the two horses she was in charge of. Then she strolled over to the far end of the stables to take another look at the cross-country course. She knew it like the back of her hand – they'd all spent ages helping Nick set it up during the winter. Although the jumps weren't all that high, the course was a challenging one and each fence would have to be jumped clear, or the horse would take a heavy rap.

"Without our own cross-country course to practise over, we won't stand a chance at Tentenden," Nick had told them.

"Hey, I've been looking for you everywhere." Jess's voice interrupted Rosie's thoughts. "Have you forgotten we've got a Tentenden training session?"

"Course not," Rosie replied. "I was just checking out the course. Let's go."

The two girls chattered excitedly as they began getting themselves ready. Rosie collected her riding hat and made her way to Pepper's stable. The little piebald sniffed the air with excitement as Rosie folded back his rug and started to tack him up. Attaching the breast plate to the saddle, she led him out of his stable to join the others.

Springing nimbly into the saddle, Rosie nudged Pepper on through the gate at the back of the yard, into the fields behind. A strong wind was blowing and it was starting to drizzle with rain, but it was still fine weather for a cross-country ride. Rosie drew Pepper to a halt under the trees.

"Here we all are then. Excited?" Beth asked, reaching for her field binoculars. "As this is the first time I've taken you over the course, I'm not going to time you. It's quite slippery, so concentrate on getting round safely. Okay?"

"Yes, Beth," they chorused.

"Let's get going before it pours down," Beth added. "Take extra care through the woods, folks, because last week's storm brought down lots of branches, and I don't want to spook your horses. Do you all know where you're going?"

"Yes, Beth," they repeated in unison.

"Great. Charlie, you go first, then Jess, Tom, and finally Rosie," Beth called.

Rosie didn't know whether to feel relieved or disappointed. She didn't want to go first, but at the same time, she could hardly bear to wait for her turn as the last one. Rosie watched closely as Charlie approached the first jump. He was so quick and skilful – she felt a twinge of jealousy.

After watching Tom ride up to the trees, Rosie

decided it was time to start warming Pepper up. She turned the little pony to a quiet corner of the field and started to trot him round. Then she pushed him on into a gentle canter. Pepper had such a smooth, rhythmical stride, he was a pleasure to ride. When she returned to the group, relaxed and ready, Jess had already finished her turn around the course, and Tom was halfway round.

"How was it, Jess?" Rosie asked.

"Brilliant!" Jess leant forward to pat Storm Cloud's neck. "Storm Cloud was amazing. Weren't you, girl?"

Then Rosie heard Beth call her name. Turning Pepper to the start, she felt the pony lengthen his stride. With a gentle squeeze of her legs, she drove him forward, and the pony jumped over the tiger trap perfectly. As Rosie steadied him before the brush, she felt a slight tremor run through his body. They took the fence easily, too, and raced on towards the hayrack.

"Steady now Pepper. Easy does it," she whispered.

Rosie sat deeper in the saddle and collected Pepper for the spread. Pepper snatched at the reins, impatiently waiting for Rosie to release him for the jump. She urged him on, letting the reins ease through her fingers as the pony jumped clear and soared over the hedge. Leaning forward as they entered the trees, Rosie swung Pepper towards the tree trunk and drove him on. Without hesitating, Pepper rose to the challenge, up and over on to the log pile.

Rosie knew they were going well. Pepper gathered his legs up under him and they flew over the tyres. Galloping forward, clear of the water jump, they approached the zigzag rails and she held her breath. They jumped it squarely and the gutsy little pony went on to race over the gate. Rosie felt herself slipping and gripped harder with her knees as they thundered across the fields. The rain was teeming down as they took the stone wall. Touchdown! They'd done it.

Pepper snorted, his breath spiralling out of his

nostrils like clouds of smoke, as Rosie slowed his pace to a trot and they went to join the others.

"Quick everyone," Beth said, "we'll have to hurry back to the yard if we don't want to get drenched."

As the horses wound their way back into the yard, Rosie was soaked through to the skin, but somehow it didn't matter. Leading Pepper into his stable, she removed his tack and started to rub him down. Then, she hurried to the tack room to collect some grooming kit. Putting her head over Blackjack's stable door, she glanced inside. Susannah – one of the younger pupils – was there with him.

"Did you enjoy your ride?" Rosie asked.

"It was great," she replied. "Alex told me I was really improving," she added proudly.

"Well done, Susannah." Rosie smiled. "If you nip to the barn and get Blackjack's food, I'll take over grooming him if you like."

"Thanks. I think my mum's waiting for me outside." Susannah skipped off to get the food.

Rosie picked up the body brush and made a start

on Blackjack's mottled coat.

"Here's his food, Rosie," Susannah called.

"Great." Rosie flashed a smile at Susannah. "See you the same time next week then."

"See you!" Susannah beamed as she ran off to find her mother.

Blackjack shifted his weight as he eyed the food sitting outside the stable, and nosed Rosie's back to remind her that he was waiting.

"I haven't forgotten you, Blackjack, but you can't have your lunch till I've got you clean." Rosie chuckled as she bent down to pick out his last hoof. Then, patting his hindquarters, she took in his food and left him munching.

This is fun, she thought. Her two horses were sorted, just as they'd planned. She hoped Jess had Storm Cloud and Minstrel settled just as quickly. After all, there were important plans to attend to before the afternoon rides.

"All set, Jess?" Rosie called out, as she saw her friend scurry past.

"I'll check on Storm Cloud and I'll be right there," Jess replied.

Five minutes later, the two friends were jogging down the lane towards the bus stop at the corner of Sandy Lane.

"Just in time!" Jess panted, as the bus pulled up. "Two halves to Colcott, please."

As they sat down inside the bus, the two girls chattered excitedly. They watched fields of greenery speed past as the bus climbed the winding road away from the coast.

Before long, the bus arrived in the town centre. Jumping off, Rosie and Jess made their way to the old saddlery.

"Afternoon, Jess... Rosie." Mr. Armstrong, the shop owner, smiled as the girls walked in.

The Sandy Lane regulars spent so much time in his shop that he knew all their names, and he was particularly fond of these two girls.

"They're ready," he said. "I hope these are what you wanted."

The girls grinned as Mr. Armstrong placed four brand new skull cap covers, in Sandy Lane red and black quarters, on the counter.

"Yes, Mr. Armstrong," Jess breathed. "Those are exactly what we wanted."

"We'll look like a real team now," Rosie added. "I can't wait to see the others' faces."

"Don't they know you've ordered them, then?" Mr. Armstrong asked.

"No," Jess replied. "Rosie and I have been saving up for them for ages. We wanted it to be a surprise."

"And how are Nick and Sarah?" Mr. Armstrong added, as he opened the till.

"Haven't you heard?" Rosie glanced anxiously at Jess. "They're away at the moment. Sarah's father's been taken ill, so they've had to go to America to run his stud farm for him. We're helping Beth look after Sandy Lane while they're away."

Mr. Armstrong looked up, concerned. "How long are they planning to be away for? Is it serious?"

"I'm afraid it is," said Rosie. "He's had a heart

attack. They're going to be away for three weeks."

"Well, if you speak to them, do send them my best wishes," Mr. Armstrong said kindly.

Rosie nodded. "Will do. Come on, Jess. We'd better get going or we'll miss the next bus back. We need to get the horses groomed and tacked up for the afternoon rides."

"Bye, Mr. Armstrong," the girls called as they left the shop.

The low rumble of the bus sounded in the distance as Rosie and Jess waited at the stop. Twenty minutes later, the girls were back at Sandy Lane.

Dashing up the drive, Rosie went straight to Pepper's stable – but it was empty.

"Uh oh," she said to herself. "Too late."

Jess looked equally sheepish when she met Rosie in the middle of the yard.

"Someone's beaten us to it, Jess," Rosie said. "We're not going to be very popular."

"We're not that late," Jess insisted. "Wait till the others see what we've got for them. They won't be angry then."

"I hope you're right." Rosie gulped, hiding the bag of skull cap covers behind her back. "Let's go and find them."

"Hi everyone," said Jess brightly, as the two girls walked into the tack room.

"Nice of you to drop by," Charlie said, returning her smile with an angry glare.

"Sorry," Rosie mumbled. "We didn't realize we'd been so long."

"Obviously." Charlie folded his arms.

"It's not very responsible to go disappearing on the first day we're in charge." Tom frowned. "We've all had to help get your horses tacked up."

"We've got to pull together while Nick and Sarah are away." Kate looked equally as cross.

"We know that," Jess cried. "We're not trying to skive. It's just that we had to collect some things."

"What things?" Charlie replied.

"These!" Rosie pulled out the bag from behind her back. "Hopefully they'll get us out of your bad books. We bought them for Tentenden."

The colourful caps spilled out onto the tack room desk, and everyone gasped.

"Well, what a great idea!" Alex smiled.

"Oh Jess, Rosie. They're perfect. You'll all look really professional," Kate exclaimed.

"Yes, thanks you two," said Tom, running the silk caps through his fingers.

"We had no idea what you two were up to." Charlie's frown was replaced with a broad grin. "They're amazing!"

Rosie smiled with relief. "I know we're all meant to be helping out, but we didn't think you'd miss us for an hour. We really wanted it to be a surprise..."

"Sorry we were angry." Tom walked over and hugged Rosie and Jess. "We really appreciate the effort. But there's still a lot to do here before we even think about Tentenden..."

"I know, I know," Rosie agreed. Then, linking arms with Jess and Tom, she led them out of the tack room. "We'd better get to it!"

Chapter 3

Disaster Strikes

"Don't let him puff out his belly when you're trying to tighten up the girth, Jess," Charlie called from the other side of the yard.

"I know that," Jess snapped. "But it's easier said than done. Why don't *you* put on Minstrel's saddle if you think you can do it any better, Charlie!"

It had only been four days since they had all waved goodbye to Nick and Sarah, and arguments were already in full swing. They quarrelled about who was taking the lead, who was in charge, who did what jobs. It was truly terrible, and Rosie was sure it was getting worse. The main problem was that nobody was in charge. She liked Beth a lot, but she just couldn't keep control in the way Nick did. They weren't getting anything done on time either. Rosie looked at her watch. It was five past eleven. Beth was supposed to have started the lesson in road-work at eleven, and Pepper was the only one of the horses tacked up. Pupils were waiting.

"Come on you lot," Rosie said. "I must have circled Pepper at least a dozen times. Let's go."

But it was another quarter of an hour before Jester, Napoleon, Minstrel, Storm Cloud and Whispering Silver were all ready to go.

"Finally," Rosie mumbled.

"Who's going on this ride, Rosie?" Beth called.

"The ones training for their road-work test – George, Melissa, Anna, Mark and me," Rosie replied.

"Excellent." Beth looked relieved. "All good, experienced riders. Follow on, everyone!"

Rosie nudged Pepper forward, relieved to be leaving the others behind her to argue things out.

Despite all the stress, Rosie felt proud as she looked at the horses' buffed coats – they were doing their best to keep things running smoothly. Perhaps they could make it work, after all... Beth and Whispering Silver led the string of horses, while Rosie took up the rear.

The further they rode from the stables, the better Rosie felt, as if by leaving the yard she had left all the arguments behind as well. She breathed in the smell of the countryside, and sighed with pleasure at the thought of all the days she would spend at Sandy Lane this Easter.

Rosie didn't know when she first heard the car coming. It all happened so quickly. One moment, they were ambling along the side of the road. The next, a sleek red sports car shot out of the Colcott junction and was heading straight for them at top speed. She collected her reins and checked Pepper, but the riders ahead were having real trouble with their frightened horses.

Any minute now the car will slow down, Rosie

thought. But if anything, the car seemed to accelerate. Rosie looked on in horror as it swerved out of control across the road, missing the horses by inches. Within seconds, horses and riders spun in a whirlwind of colours, as the sound of shrieks and panic-stricken hooves merged as one.

Storm Cloud pirouetted in staccato movements, cannoning into the other stampeding horses. Then Whispering Silver reared, her eyes rolling in sheer terror, her legs flailing around in the air as Beth clung on for dear life. In a split second, Whispering Silver's shoes struck the ground and Beth was flung sideways. There was a sickening crunch as she hit the ground. Whispering Silver thundered off down the road, and most of the other horses and their riders followed him, all of them completely out of control. Suddenly, Rosie snapped to her senses.

"Pull on the reins! Try to turn them back!" Rosie shouted after them. But it was too late. Napoleon was the only horse left behind, and George was struggling to control him. Rosie jumped down from

Pepper and ran over to Beth, who lay on the ground, not moving, with one leg twisted awkwardly under her body.

"Is she dead?" George whispered, as he tugged on Napoleon's reins.

"No," said Rosie, shakily. "I can feel a pulse, and she's breathing. But we need an ambulance now." She pulled out her mobile and began to dial. After a short pause, she looked up at George in panic. "No signal!" she cried. "Do you have any?"

George pulled out his mobile, then shook his head. "No! What shall we do?"

"You'll have to ride down the road until you find some. I'll stay here with Beth." Rosie gently shook Beth's shoulders. "Beth? Beth?" she said. But her words were met with silence, and Beth didn't stir.

George leaped down from Napoleon and tied Pepper's reins to a tree. Then he jumped back on to the little bay and turned him up the road towards Ash Hill.

"Call Tom at Sandy Lane too," Rosie shouted after

him. "Get him to come out and look for the others. And hurry!"

As Napoleon galloped into the distance, Rosie bent over Beth, and began stroking her hair softly. "You're going to be all right," Rosie whispered. "Please, please be all right."

It had started to rain, but Rosie took off her coat and laid it over Beth to keep her warm and dry. Rosie felt so helpless, just waiting.

"Beth... Beth can you hear me?" Rosie tried again.

Beth opened one eye and groaned faintly. "It's... it's my leg," she murmured.

Rosie's heart leaped at the sound of Beth's voice. "I know," she soothed. "Try not to move it. Help is coming soon."

She looked at her watch. It could only have been five minutes ago that George had left, but it felt like hours. Where was he? Where was the ambulance? A few more minutes passed, when suddenly she heard the sound of a horse cantering towards them. It was George on Napoleon.

"The ambulance is on its way." The words tumbled out of George's mouth. "I managed to get a signal and phoned Tom... He's coming out with Alex on foot... How is she?"

"She's come round," Rosie said. "Her leg's hurting her, but I..." She stopped when she heard the sound of a siren, getting louder and louder.

"The ambulance!" George cried, jumping off Napoleon to wave them down.

Within seconds, the ambulance had pulled up by the roadside, neon lights flashing. Then, three paramedics jumped out and rushed over to Rosie and Beth.

"What's her name?" One of the paramedics bent down next to Beth.

"Beth. She's called Beth." Rosie answered, watching as the other two unloaded a stretcher from the ambulance.

"Pulse is okay," the paramedic murmured. "Temperature okay."

Rosie felt a wave of relief flood through her.

"Do you hurt anywhere, Beth?" The paramedic leant in closely as Beth groaned, and mumbled something incoherent.

"She said something about her leg," Rosie replied.

"I see." The paramedic motioned to one of the others to fetch something.

Rosie watched as they attached a support bandage to Beth's leg and then gently rolled her onto a board and carried her over to the stretcher.

"What happens now?" Rosie asked desperately.

"We're taking her to Barkston hospital," the paramedic said. "Do you have a phone number for her family?"

"Yes, I think so." Rosie scrolled through her mobile to find the number.

"I'll radio the hospital and get them to call out the police," said the paramedic. "Wait till they get here – they'll tell you what to do."

Rosie and George watched as the paramedics jumped into the ambulance and drove off. Then they stood on the roadside, waiting anxiously.

"Tom and the others should be here any moment," George said, as Napoleon nuzzled his side. "In fact, there they are now."

Rosie turned to look back in the direction of Sandy Lane to see Tom and Alex racing towards them. "Thank goodness," she cried.

"Is Beth okay?" Tom panted, catching his breath.

"She's been taken to Barkston hospital, but she was conscious," Rosie replied. "I think she may have broken her leg – she was in a lot of pain."

"Are you all right Rosie? George?" Alex looked at them both, concerned.

"Yes, we're just shocked. It was all so quick." Rosie shook her head. "The car didn't stop, or even slow down. Beth could have been killed..."

"Idiot driver," Tom snapped. "Did you get a number plate?"

"No." Rosie gazed in the direction that the car had gone. "But it was a man, and the car was a red sports car. I can remember that much."

"What about you, George?" Tom asked.

"I'm afraid it was all a blur for me," George answered, shaking his head.

"Right, we've got to find the others," said Tom. "Which way did they go?"

Rosie pointed vaguely in the direction of Ash Hill. "I've no idea how far they got..."

"Don't worry. We'll find them." Tom took Napoleon's reins from George. "We'll take Pepper and Napoleon off your hands – it'll be quicker on them. You wait here for the police."

Rosie and George watched as the two boys mounted the horses and cantered into the distance. Not long after, sirens flashed as a police car arrived.

"I'm PC Dale," a police officer said, climbing out of the car. "The hospital radioed that there had been an accident. Can you tell me what happened?"

"Yes of course," Rosie said. "The ambulance has taken Beth off – she was thrown from her horse."

"Where are the other riders I was told about?" the police officer asked.

"The horses bolted with their riders. Our friends

have already gone to look for them... We were just waiting for you..." Rosie stammered.

"I won't keep you long." The police officer smiled kindly as she pulled out a notepad. "I just need a few details, then I'll run you back to the stables. So where did the car come from then?" she began.

"The Colcott junction, over there," Rosie replied.

"But it didn't actually hit anyone?"

"No," Rosie said hesitantly. "But it was going extremely fast."

"And where were the horses on the road?" the police officer continued.

"In single file," Rosie said. "We were practising for our road safety exams, so we wouldn't have ridden any other way."

"That's good." PC Dale nodded approvingly. "And how many people were there in the vehicle?"

"Just one – a man I think," Rosie answered. "But I didn't get a clear view of him."

"What about you – did you see?" PC Dale turned to George.

"I was too busy trying to hold my horse steady," George said.

"And neither of you got the registration number?"

"No, sorry," Rosie said. She was suddenly very tired. "Is that all you need to know?"

Rosie watched as PC Dale scribbled one last thing down and snapped her notepad shut. "That's all for now," the police officer said. "I'll take you back now."

"Do you think you'll find the driver?" George asked, as they drove back towards the stables along the winding roads.

"To be honest, it's tricky, as the car didn't actually hit anything..." PC Dale admitted.

"But it was obvious the man drove far too close to us," George interrupted.

"That may be so," PC Dale went on. "But it'll be difficult to prove, and without a vehicle registration number it's unlikely we'll be able to trace him."

Rosie stared dejectedly out of the window, thinking about the selfish driver, and poor Beth, lying in hospital in pain. That car had definitely speeded up; it had been no accident. As the police car turned into the drive of Sandy Lane, Rosie winced as she remembered the moment Beth flew off her horse and landed on the ground. What on earth were they going to tell Nick and Sarah?

Chapter 4

Holding the Fort

"I suppose it could have been worse," Charlie whispered. "At least all the other riders are safe, and none of the horses are injured."

It was late afternoon, and the Sandy Lane regulars were all huddled in the tack room listening to Tom on the phone to Beth's mother.

"It's as Rosie suspected," said Tom, putting down the phone. "Beth's broken her leg, and the hospital reckon it will take at last six weeks to heal. She has to stay at home until she's fully recovered."

"Who's going to run Sandy Lane?" Rosie asked.

"Don't worry, Rosie," Tom replied. "I'm going to ring Nick's friend Dick Bryant now. That's what he told us to do if we were really stuck."

He dialled the number, and waited patiently. "No answer," he said, finally.

"We'll have to phone Nick and Sarah, then." Rosie ran her fingers through her hair, feeling worried.

"No," said Tom. "I don't want to worry them if we don't have to. They've got enough to think about as it is. We'll pack things up here tonight, then try Dick again tomorrow."

"But what about tomorrow's lessons?" Rosie went on. "Shouldn't we cancel them?"

"No... not yet," Tom replied. "We'll manage. It's only for a day. I can always take over Beth's lessons and then we'll divide the hacks between us. We'll get hold of him tomorrow, and it will be fine."

"Unless we run Sandy Lane ourselves," Charlie suggested. "I'm sure we could manage until Nick and Sarah get back..."

"Don't even think about it," Tom said, sharply.

"We can't possibly do that. Nick would go mad."

"I suppose you're right." Charlie shrugged. "It was just an idea. You must admit, it would be fun."

"Fun, but stupid." Tom was firm. "But we can hold the fort until tomorrow. If we're all agreed, there are twelve hungry horses waiting to be fed."

Alex nodded. "I'll nip across to the cottage and turn some lights on, so our parents don't suspect anything when they drop us off."

"Good idea," Tom said. "That way nobody will try to contact Nick. Right, guys. For one day only, we're in charge!"

Rosie felt uneasy. She didn't like keeping things from her parents, but she didn't want to say so. Still, it was only for a day, after all.

The next morning passed uneventfully at Sandy Lane. Unfortunately, every time Tom called Dick Bryant, there was no answer. At a quarter to two, the regulars met in the tack room to delegate tasks.

"Right, time to sort this afternoon out," Tom said. "I'll take that private lesson. Rosie and Jess – do you think you could take the two o'clock hack out?"

"Of course!" said Rosie, excitedly. It was the hack that went to the lighthouse – her favourite ride. She rushed off to Pepper's stable.

A few minutes later, Jess's head appeared over the stable door. "Rosie, can you help David Taylor mount Blackjack? His mother is dropping him off for his private lesson."

"Sure!" Rosie followed Jess outside. "Hello Mrs. Taylor. Hi David." Rosie smiled at the pair who were waiting in the yard. "Tom's taking David's lesson this afternoon. I hope that's okay for you both."

"Tom's taking it?" Mrs. Taylor looked surprised. "But where's Beth?"

"I'm afraid she's had an accident," Rosie replied. "She was knocked off her horse by a car."

"Is she all right?" Mrs. Taylor looked concerned.

"She's broken her leg," Rosie said. "She'll be off for six weeks."

"Oh dear, poor girl." Mrs. Taylor hesitated. "Are you sure Tom is up to lessons?"

"Yes. He's an excellent rider, and it's only for today – some of Nick's friends are coming to help tomorrow," said Rosie, hoping it was true.

"Well, I suppose if it's only for today. And Tom is a good rider..." Mrs. Taylor looked unsure.

"The best," Rosie said, firmly.

"If Nick trusts him, I'm sure it will be all right." Mrs. Taylor looked at her son. "Is that okay, David?"

The little boy nodded excitedly, and Rosie helped him into the saddle. Then she circled the pony around the yard until Tom arrived.

"Hi David," Tom called. "Are you ready?"

"Great. I'll be back at three," Mrs. Taylor said, getting into her car. "Have fun!"

Rosie watched as Tom and David set off to the outdoor school for the lesson. Then she hurried back to Pepper's stable and, after tacking him up, led him out to join the other riders who had gathered in the yard ready for the hack.

There was a girl from the year below her at school on Minstrel, a boy with dark hair riding Hector, a blonde girl she didn't recognize with Jester, and Jess was on Storm Cloud. Excitedly, the riders wound their way out of the yard. Jess headed the line and Rosie brought up the rear. The horses trotted happily down the drive and into the lane.

"Right, let's have a canter," Jess called from the front. "All meet up over there, by those trees."

Rosie waited for the other horses to set off and then, with a little nudge of her heels, she pushed Pepper on. She sat tight to the saddle as they headed for the trees together. Nothing made her feel as good as riding did, she decided at that moment.

An hour later, at the end of the hack, they all wound their way back to Sandy Lane together.

"How was David's lesson, Tom?" Rosie called, as she led Pepper back into his stable.

"Went really well, actually," Tom answered. "I never thought I'd have the patience."

Rosie smiled. Anyone with enough patience to spend a whole summer training a horse, as Tom had trained Chancey, was bound to be a good teacher.

Why hadn't he realised it before, she wondered.

"There's a meeting in the tack room in five minutes," Jess called over to her.

Hurrying into the tack room with Pepper's saddle slung over her arm, Rosie joined the others.

"Okay everyone," Tom said. "Still no response from Dick Bryant – he must be away. I'll keep trying, but I think we have to make a group decision here. I think we should wait one more day. We can cope can't we? I think things have run pretty smoothly so far today. Do you all agree?"

"Definitely," said Jess, and the others nodded.

"Good," said Tom. "Then we're agreed. If we don't hear from Dick by tomorrow, we really do have to phone Nick and Sarah."

The thought of spending another day running Sandy Lane with her friends was wonderful, and Rosie went home buzzing with excitement. Today had gone so well, and tomorrow could be even better, now they were organised. *What a fantastic team they made*, she thought as she cycled home.

Chapter 5

The Newcomers

Rosie got to the yard early the next day. It was a cold, crisp spring morning and all was peaceful at Sandy Lane. *Another great day ahead*, she thought.

"Morning, Storm Cloud," she called as the dappled grey pony peered over her stable door to greet her.

She hurried over to the tack room to look at the appointments book. Three hacks and two lessons: nothing they couldn't handle. Then, she found the key to Nick and Sarah's cottage and went over to let out their black Labrador, Ebony, after a long night on her own.

"All right, you daft dog." Rosie laughed as Ebony jumped up. "You'll have your breakfast in a moment."

As she reached up to get Ebony's food, she looked out of the window and saw a tall, wiry man walking up the drive. She ignored him at first, but when she looked again, he was grinding out his cigarette on the ground with his boot. Rosie was annoyed. You should never smoke in or around stables, not with all the hay and straw around. She didn't like the look of this man, or what he was doing. Was he here for a lesson, or to deliver something? Rushing out of the cottage, she approached the stranger.

"Can I help you?" she asked, with more politeness than she felt. The man spun round, startled.

"Well, I'm here to help you, actually," he said, narrowing his eyes. "I'm a friend of Nick and Sarah's."

Rosie looked puzzled.

"Nick and Sarah Brooks?" the man went on. "The stable owners?"

"Of course," said Rosie, flustered by his rude tone.

"It's just that we weren't expecting anyone today..."

"Well, Nick called me yesterday. He told me about Beth's accident and asked me to come along and help out. I got here as quickly as I could."

"Oh, right," said Rosie, with relief. "You must be Dick Bryant. Nick left us your number. We've been trying to get hold of you for the last two days..."

"No, I'm Sam Durant, actually," the man said quickly. "Dick's away at the moment, so Nick has asked me to help out instead."

Rosie tried to make sense of it all. "So Nick knows about the accident, does he?" she asked.

"Yes, I think your stable girl called him," the man said, turning away.

"What did he say? Are they coming back?"

"Well, of course Nick was worried," the man replied. "But he called Vanessa and me in to help out. He trusts us to do a good job."

"Vanessa?" Rosie said. This didn't feel right at all.

"My wife," he said. "Nick said we could live in the cottage while we're here."

"Well, I'm sure there won't be a problem, but I think you'd better talk to Tom and the others about that." Rosie knew how rude this sounded, but there was something about this man she really didn't like. If he was planning to move into Nick and Sarah's home, the others should definitely be told...

"Of course there won't be a problem, my dear." The man smirked. "It's all been sorted out, so there's nothing to talk about, is there?"

Rosie felt uneasy as he turned away again.

"Vanessa and I will be back at two o'clock to move in," he called over his shoulder.

"Wait!" she shouted after him. But he ignored her, and disappeared down the drive.

Rosie picked up a broom and started to sweep the yard. She couldn't stop thinking about Sam Durant, and how awful he was. But if he and his wife were going to be running Sandy Lane, it wasn't a good idea to fall out with them. Nick might trust him with the stables, but she didn't, so she needed to stay alert. She was relieved when the others arrived.

Immediately, she began telling them about him.

"What was he like?" Jess asked, when Rosie had finished explaining.

"Horrible," Rosie said.

"In what way?" Tom asked.

"Well," Rosie hesitated. "It's hard to describe. There was just something odd about him. I suppose I just don't like the idea of strangers coming in and running Sandy Lane."

"Look," Tom replied authoritatively. "I think it's only fair to give them a few days to settle in. It's a big thing running a stables, and if Nick's got Sam in to help, we can't send him away just because Rosie doesn't like him."

"Tom's right, Rosie," Jess said quietly.

"Yes... Maybe they are awful, but we should probably put up with them," Charlie agreed.

Rosie sighed. "Okay, whatever you guys think."

"Let's show them how we do things in Sandy Lane, and then he can tell Nick and Sarah that we've done a great job," Tom said. "There's work to be done, so let's do it."

Everyone nodded in agreement, and Jess and Rosie headed off to start the mucking out. By half past eight, twelve horses had been mucked out, groomed and fed.

"Right, when's today's first lesson?" Jess said, coming into the tack room.

"Nine o'clock," Rosie answered. "Tom's taking a private lesson and you and I are taking out the hack."

"Cool," said Jess. "It'll be good to get out in the fresh air after all those smelly stables!"

As everyone got to work, the morning passed by in a flash. Two o'clock came and went, but there was no sign of Sam and Vanessa Durant. It wasn't until a quarter past five that a white Range Rover pulled up in the yard. Sam Durant jumped out, followed by a stylish woman clad in designer black jodhpurs and a silk scarf, knotted at her neck.

"Wow! They're not how I imagined them to be, Rosie," Tom whispered.

"A bit too trendy for horsy people." Rosie scowled.

"Horsy people don't have to look scruffy, Rosie," Jess replied. "They look important."

Sam strode straight over to Tom, ignoring the two girls completely.

"You must be Tom," he said grandly. "I've heard great things about you. I'm Sam Durant, an old riding friend of Nick's."

"Nice to meet you," said Tom, blushing with pride at Sam's praise.

"And this is my wife, Vanessa," Sam continued, introducing the woman beside him.

Rosie watched as her friends queued up to introduce themselves. She still felt unsure about this man, however impressed the others were.

After they'd finished the introductions, Sam turned to the group. "Well, you lot seem to have been managing things just fine here. How have you been doing it?"

"We've each been responsible for looking after two horses, and then we take turns in leading hacks," Tom explained. "And I've taken Beth's lessons for the last couple of days," he went on. "I know I shouldn't have, really, but..."

"Perfect," Sam said, breezily. "We'll continue in the same way. You can do the morning lessons, Tom, and I'll do the lessons in the afternoon."

Tom beamed, but Rosie couldn't believe what she was hearing.

"But Tom, you're not qualified to take lessons," she whispered.

"Shhh," Tom hissed. "If Sam thinks I'm up to it, I'm up to it." He smiled at Sam. "Fine with me, Sam."

"Right... all settled?" Sam went on. "I'm more than happy with that arrangement."

"I bet you are," Rosie muttered. "It means less work for you."

"Vanessa will be booking in the rides," Sam said.

"What about our Tentenden training sessions?" Jess asked, anxiously.

"Are you entered for the Tentenden Team Chase?" Sam looked vaguely annoyed.

"Yes," Jess said. "Nick has already picked us four

to represent Sandy Lane." She indicated herself, Tom, Charlie and Rosie. "And we've set up a programme of training sessions."

"Well I'll take over those sessions then," Sam said briskly. "We'll be settling in if anyone wants us," he added, as he and Vanessa walked away.

Rosie scowled at their retreating backs.

"Don't be like that, Rosie," Jess said crossly. "They seem okay to me."

"I don't know why you've taken this instant dislike to them," Tom added. "It sounds as if they're not going to bother us too much. They'll leave us to do pretty much as we like, and he'll help with Tentenden. It's perfect."

"There's something not quite right about them," Rosie insisted.

"You've been watching too many crime dramas!" Tom teased. "Stop being so paranoid, Rosie."

A few minutes later, the phone rang in the tack room. Tom picked it up: it was Beth's mother.

"Yes Mrs. Wilson," Tom was saying, as everybody

crowded around him. "We're fine... No, we didn't get hold of Dick Bryant, but Nick and Sarah have sent some other friends in to run the stables. They seem great. How's Beth doing? Can she have visitors yet? ... No, I understand – we'll wait until she's feeling more up to it. Tell her to get better soon."

Rosie looked at her watch. She'd have to hurry – her mum wanted her home for six. As she crossed the room to the door, all eyes were on Tom as they listened carefully to what he was saying.

"Bye everyone," Rosie called, but no one replied. Rosie shrugged her shoulders and slipped out through the door. For the first time ever, Rosie felt like an outsider at the stables – and it felt horrible.

Chapter 6

Standards Slip

From the moment Sam and Vanessa took over, the Sandy Lane regulars were extremely busy. There was so much to do – hacks to organize, lessons to take, and they had no time to fit in any training for the Tentenden Team Chase. In four days, Sam only took them over the cross-country course once.

"But that was the deal, wasn't it?" Tom said one day. "I take lessons in the morning, he takes lessons in the afternoon and we all help around the yard."

"They aren't doing much of anything that I can see," Rosie said.

"Give them a chance, Rosie. Sam says he's an expert on cross-country," Tom snapped. "We can learn a lot from him."

"Well I'm not learning much," she replied. "He's too busy talking about himself to teach us anything. And it's the yard I'm worried about, not his riding skills," she continued. "Vanessa's useless at the bookings – she can't understand the online system. Nick and Sarah will lose money if she doesn't get her act together. Melissa even said she might try lessons at the Clarendon Equestrian Centre instead!"

"What! That place has only been open six months, and it's already got a bad reputation." Tom frowned. "The horses look all right, but they're really badly schooled. I heard that the owner, Ralph Winterson, is never there. He leaves the stable girls and boys to do everything, apparently."

"And he's been done for cruelty to horses in the past," Alex added. "I heard he had to close down his last stables for rapping. He only got away with it because it was his word against a little girl's, but everyone knew he'd been lifting the poles to get her horse to jump higher."

"Hmm." Rosie paused. "Whatever's gone on at Clarendon, we're stuck with Sam Durant, and I need him to sign the Tentenden entry form. If someone doesn't post it today, we'll miss the closing date!"

She headed off to a quiet corner to fill out the form. *Perhaps I'd better keep my opinions of Sam and Vanessa to myself*, she thought. Everybody else seemed to think they were wonderful.

A while later, Jess came to find her. "Rosie, we've had an email from Nick and Sarah. Come and have a look!"

Rosie jumped up and followed Jess into the office.

"Dear all," Jess read out. "Arrived safely. Sarah's dad is improving slowly. We're very busy here, but should still be back on the 20th as planned. We'd send you some photos, but the internet connection here is terrible! See you soon. Love Nick and Sarah."

"That's weird. They must have written that before Beth's accident," said Rosie. "Sam told me that Beth had told them about it herself. I guess if the internet's bad where they are, the email probably got held up in the outbox and didn't send."

"Guess so, otherwise they'd have asked how Beth is," Jess replied. "Anyway, it doesn't matter. Sam says he'll take us over the cross-country course today – now that is important."

"Cross-country?" Rosie said puzzled. "I didn't know we had training this morning. Is Sam up and about then? Bit early for him, isn't it?"

Jess laughed. "Yes he is, I saw him just now. He says he'll take Kate and Alex too, not just the team for Tentenden."

Rosie walked out into the yard, leaving the application form on the desk. Some practice for the competition, at last! Tom was leading Whispering Silver out of her stable.

"Where are you going with Whisp, Tom?" she called out.

"Sam wants to try her over the cross-country," Tom answered.

"What? But Nick doesn't let anyone ride Whisp over the course," said Rosie. "Her legs aren't up to it, not if she takes a heavy rap. She's getting older now. Nick wants us to be careful with her."

"Sam thinks it'll strengthen her legs, and he's going to jump her carefully, Rosie." Tom looked angry. "Why are you always questioning his judgement? Stop getting at him, will you? I'm sure he knows better than any of us what her legs can and can't take. He's the expert, not you, remember?"

Rosie turned away to hide the tears in her eyes. Leading Pepper out to join the others, she shivered as a gust of wind blew across the yard. She was not looking forward to this session any more, but she had to hide her feelings.

"Is everyone here?" Sam asked, opening the gate to the fields at the back. "Everyone gather over by the big beech tree."

The horses trotted over to the tree and stopped in a group, as Sam cantered over to join them.

"Okay. Let's get going," Sam called. "And

remember, speed is the key."

Rosie felt uneasy straight away. Why was 'speed the key'? It was vital, but surely care and safety were important too? She had never been intimidated by the cross-country course before – never doubted her own ability – until today, with Sam in charge.

"I'll go round once to show you how it's done," Sam said briskly. "Then I'll watch you one by one. This is your time to convince me that you're the right choice for the Tentenden team," he said, looking directly at Rosie.

"Did you hear that?" she whispered to Jess. "He wants me out of the team."

"Don't be silly, Rosie." Jess rolled her eyes. "It wasn't aimed at you. I'm sure Sam wouldn't alter the team now... Not after all the training we've put in. It's just his way of keeping us on our toes."

"I hope you're right," Rosie said, miserably. But she didn't feel convinced.

Rosie watched Sam turn Whispering Silver towards the first fence with a crack from his whip.

The horse stumbled and hurtled towards the tiger trap at breakneck speed as Sam crouched low onto her neck, his legs tucked neatly beneath him. They careered over the jump and, as they landed, Sam pushed her on still more. Whisp responded bravely, picking up speed until she battled her way over the next jump and then they went out of sight and into the woods.

"Wow. They're going so fast," Jess cried. "Hey, are you all right, Rosie?"

"Yes," Rosie breathed, but she felt sick and her face had gone ghostly-white. She knew that Sam was asking too much of Whisp and that Nick would be devastated if anything happened to that horse. Why was nobody saying anything?

Then, horse and rider charged out of the trees and headed for the next jump. They skimmed it and plunged into the water, but Whisp was sinking, her legs thrashing about until she managed to stagger up the bank, exhausted.

Rosie held her breath as they rode over the zigzag

rails, the gate, and onto the stone wall. Whisp was in a lather, her body bathed in sweat, and she was quivering. Sam's jodhpurs were splattered with mud all the way up.

"That was fast, Sam. It looked amazing." Tom's face was full of awe.

"It was," Sam said, coolly. "Now you try. I had a bit of trouble in the woods, though. I think the old horse took a bit of a rap."

Rosie looked down at Whispering Silver's delicate legs, but Sam was clicking his stopwatch for Tom's ride rather than seeing if the horse was badly hurt.

Rosie had never seen her friend go so fast. She was worried that it could strain Chancey's heart… but he was Tom's horse, after all. Thundering over the tiger trap, they raced to the brush hurdle. Chancey hardly seemed to touch the ground as he cleared all the jumps, and then came out of the woods and approached the water jump. But no sooner was he over it and out of the water, than Tom was pressing him on to the zigzag rails. Chancey tore over them, straining at the bit as he surged on to the low gate and, lastly, the stone wall.

Sam clicked his stop watch. "Good job," he said, as Tom returned to the group.

Rosie couldn't believe her ears. It certainly hadn't been 'a good job' – it had been bordering on dangerous. And, as she had volunteered to go last, now she would have to watch another four of her friends ride crazily around the course before she had to do it.

Rosie turned Pepper away from the group, trying to keep her calm. She tried to relax as she loosened him up, but she knew that if she aimed for speed, her style would suffer. She couldn't bear to watch the others, so when her turn came, she had no idea how they'd done. She circled Pepper, and then Sam nodded his head and she nudged the little pony forward. She turned him to the start and pushed him on into a canter.

"FASTER!" Sam roared.

As Rosie urged Pepper on, he tried to put in an

extra stride as he headed for the tiger trap and stumbled over the fence. Rosie knew she had misdirected him, and now her arms and legs were all wrong as she tugged at Pepper's reins in an effort to slow him down. Hurtling over the brush hurdle, they bounded on to the hayrack.

Pepper was excited now and snorted impatiently. Rolling his eyes, he surged ahead and for the next two jumps, Rosie found herself hanging behind. They thundered off into the woods, snagging on the low branches of trees.

She was slipping in the saddle now, and didn't know how she managed to stay on over the tyres. When the little pony checked himself at the water jump, Rosie almost flew over his head. Splashing on through the water, Rosie lost a stirrup. Desperately trying to regain her seat, she found herself completely off-balance for the next two fences and was shaking when she joined the rest of the group. It had been a terrible round.

"Not bad," said Sam, clicking his stop watch.

"Good pace, Rosie," said Jess. "If we all go that speed at Tentenden, we'll be in with a real chance."

Rosie stared at her friend. Hadn't Jess seen how badly she'd ridden? She didn't dare say anything, though – she had to be on that team.

Back in the stable, Rosie gently untacked Pepper and began to sponge him down.

"I won't let Sam spoil Tentenden for us, Pepper," she whispered to the little horse. When she had finished, she picked up the application form and went to find Sam at the cottage to sign it.

"I've got the entry form for Tentenden here," Rosie said to Sam, as he opened the front door of the cottage. "Do you think you could sign it before I nip out and post it? It needs to go off today to make sure it gets there for Friday."

"Just leave it with me, Rosie. I'll sign it and make sure it's sent off," Sam said, smoothly.

But Sam wouldn't meet Rosie's eyes, and Rosie felt uneasy. He hadn't said anything about her losing her place on the team, but she didn't trust him.

Would he leave her name on the form, or would he sneak in someone else's? She didn't dare ask – she just wasn't sure she wanted to hear the answer.

Chapter 7

From Bad to Worse

Rosie didn't sleep well that night. She had awful nightmares, full of horses falling and thrashing about in icy water. Tossing and turning, she woke up in a cold sweat. She looked at her watch: six o'clock. Dragging herself out of bed, she tugged on her jodhpurs. Today had to be better than yesterday, she decided. Nothing could possibly be worse, could it?

Ten minutes later, she was on her bike on the way to Sandy Lane. The air felt heavy with rain, as if everything in the countryside was just waiting for it to start. Turning into the drive, she propped her bike against the water trough and walked over to Whisp's stable.

At first, Rosie couldn't see anything, but once her eyes had grown accustomed to the dark, she could see the shape of the horse lying on the floor. Whisp looked up and struggled to her feet: her back offside leg was very swollen.

"Sam Durant, you idiot," Rosie muttered through gritted teeth.

Drawing back the bolt on the door, she went into the box.

"It's okay, Whisp. You're going to be all right," she whispered. The horse turned her face towards her and snickered softly. When Rosie ran her hand down the horse's leg, it was hot.

"You need the vet, you poor old thing," she said.

Rosie rang the vet, and waited in the tack room for the others to arrive. As soon as they did, she told them what had happened.

"Oh," said Tom sheepishly. "Poor Whisp. Sam did take her round pretty fast. I suppose we'd better cancel her rides for today."

Rosie headed off to check the bookings. She opened up the appointments calendar on the laptop, only to find that today's page was completely empty.

"Tom, can you come here," she called. "Do you know anything about this?"

"Where can all the bookings have gone?" he said. "It's our only record of who's riding who. How will we ever work it out now? Can you remember?"

"Not really. I know that Melissa White's on Pepper at some time but that's about it. Vanessa's the only person who might know," she said.

"What might I know?" a voice came from behind.

Rosie turned round, to see Vanessa standing in the doorway.

Tom pointed at the laptop screen. "Today's appointments have been completely wiped. There's nothing there."

"Maybe the system crashed or something," Vanessa said quickly.

"Well, we need to try and work out the bookings

sharpish," Rosie said frostily, "or today will be chaos."

"Hmm, I might be able to remember. Give me ten minutes," Vanessa said calmly. "It's that stupid online system – it probably wiped itself. I'm sure I can put a list together now."

"That would be great, thanks, Vanessa." Tom looked relieved. "Oh, that must be the vet," he added, as a car pulled up in the yard.

"The vet? What's going on?" Vanessa asked, her eyes wide.

"Didn't you know? Whisp is ill," Rosie snapped, marching off to meet the vet before Vanessa could answer. Tom hurried over to join Rosie.

"Where's the patient then?" the vet asked.

"In here," said Tom, drawing back the bolt to Whisp's box.

The two friends poked their heads over the stable door as the vet looked at the injured horse.

"She's taken a bit of a knock. There's a small cut above the fetlock. It's nothing serious, but she must rest," the vet said, patting her neck. "I'll bandage it up and leave you some Gamgee bandages to keep it clean. Make sure she isn't ridden."

Once the vet had finished bandaging Whisp, she left. Then Vanessa arrived, waving a piece of paper. "Here we are," she said. "Everything's sorted now."

"Hardly sorted," Rosie muttered, "when Whisp is still lame and she can't be ridden..."

Vanessa smiled, showing a row of perfect white teeth. "Well, it's all hacks today and no lessons, so you should be all right."

"*We* should be all right?" Now it was Tom's turn to look shocked.

"Didn't Sam tell you he was away today? He's got things to sort." Vanessa shrugged.

"I think we should get in touch with Nick and Sarah." Rosie looked at Tom anxiously. "They'd want to know what's going on with Whisp."

"Oh, I wouldn't trouble them." Vanessa stepped in quickly. "Sam spoke to Nick last night. He said Nick sounded exhausted."

Tom nodded. "I guess we don't want to worry

them. Don't you think, Rosie?"

Rosie sighed. "I suppose they've got a lot to deal with at the moment. If we can sort things out ourselves, that's probably best..."

"Well that's agreed, then," Vanessa said quickly. "I'm off shopping now – I can trust you two to look after the yard, can't I?"

"Guess so," Tom said, reading Vanessa's list with a frown. Storm Cloud, Feather, Napoleon and Minstrel had to be ready for the ten o'clock hack for the experienced riders. There was a lot to do.

"Are you listening, everyone?" Rosie called as Vanessa drove out of the yard. "We haven't got much time – fifteen minutes to get four horses ready – so let's make it snappy."

By two minutes to ten, the four horses were tacked up and waiting, eager and ready for the hack.

But ten o'clock came and no one arrived. The regulars waited and waited. After all, people were sometimes late, they told themselves. But by ten thirty, there was still no sign of anyone and Rosie was fuming.

At eleven o'clock, the riders eventually arrived, and Rosie's heart sank. They were all novices, and none of the ponies waiting were novice mounts. Vanessa had got it completely wrong.

"Oh, isn't Blackjack ready?" Mrs. Taylor asked, surprised to see Jess lead Storm Cloud out from her stable for David to ride.

"Er, I'm afraid we're a little behind this morning," Rosie said. "Whisp's lame and there seems to be a bit of a mix-up with mounts."

"Not another mix-up!" Mrs. Taylor groaned. "This is getting ridiculous. I pay a lot of money for these lessons. And where's Sam this morning? Does he know how often this keeps on happening?"

"I should think so, as he's to blame for it," Rosie muttered. "If you could give us another five minutes..." She smiled sweetly. "We're almost there."

The regulars met up in the tack room to decide what to do. Jess led the unwanted ponies back to their stables, while the others got the novice mounts ready. Rosie went to Blackjack's stable, but when she went to find his saddle, it was missing.

"Jess, have you seen Blackjack's saddle?" she called across the yard.

"No, sorry," Jess replied. "But I'll help you look."

The two friends hunted high and low, but it was nowhere to be found.

"What are we going to do?" said Rosie. "We can't put Blackjack in another saddle. It'll rub him raw with his hollow back. That saddle was made especially for him – it cost a fortune! Nick will go bonkers if it's lost."

"Come on you two. What are you up to?" Tom called into the tack room.

"Blackjack's saddle has disappeared," Jess cried.

"It can't have," Tom said. "It was there yesterday."

"Well it has." Rosie thought for a moment. "David will have to ride Horace instead. But who's going to tell his mother?"

"I will," Tom offered. He walked out of the tack room to find Mrs. Taylor. "I'm really sorry," Tom said, "but would David mind riding Horace today?"

"Where's Blackjack?" the little boy wailed, looking at his mother. "I always ride Blackjack!"

"I'm sorry." Mrs. Taylor frowned at Tom. "David only has one riding lesson a week and he adores that pony. He won't be happy to ride another horse."

"I do understand," said Tom, looking embarrassed.

She had every right to complain, Rosie thought, as Mrs. Taylor led her son back to the car. It all looked very unprofessional.

Things got no better as the day went on. Vanessa's list was worse than no list at all. Pupils booked in for private lessons were down for hacks, horses had been double-booked, rides had been mysteriously cancelled. The day was a complete disaster, and as the last hack drew to a close and the horses ate their evening feeds, they all breathed a huge sigh of relief.

But they still hadn't found Blackjack's saddle. If it didn't turn up by the morning, they'd have to order another one. The stables couldn't afford to have him missing lessons, either, especially with Whisp lame.

They counted their takings, which were much lower than usual – for the third day in a row.

Rosie didn't like to voice her doubts again, but the sooner Nick and Sarah came back the better, as far as she was concerned.

It took Rosie three days to pluck up the courage to phone the Tentenden office to find out which riders Sam had entered on the team. Had he left her name on the form? She had to know.

"Hi there," she said. "Rosie from Sandy Lane Stables here. I wondered if I could possibly check the names on our entry form, please."

"Certainly, Rosie – I'll have a look at our records," the receptionist replied. The line went quiet, and it seemed ages before the voice returned.

"I don't seem to have an entry for that name, I'm afraid," the receptionist said, finally.

"What?" Rosie gasped. "Are you quite sure?"

"Positive. We haven't had any entry come in from Sandy Lane. I've searched our emails, too."

Rosie swallowed. "So what can we do now?"

"Well, I'm afraid you've missed the deadline. You'll have to apply earlier next year."

As Rosie put the phone down, her head was spinning. So there would be no Tentenden Team Chase for any of them this year? Did the form get lost? Or... had Sam not posted it at all? Suddenly, she was sure this was what had happened. She rushed outside to tell everyone.

"You're never going to believe this," she spluttered, finding them all in the yard. "The Tentenden Office has no record of our entry for the Chase. They say they've never received the form, and now it's too late for us to enter at all."

"What?" Tom gasped. "It must be a mistake."

"The only mistake was letting Sam post our entry form," Rosie snapped.

"Let's find Sam," Tom said. "Come on."

The team trooped up to the cottage and knocked on the front door.

"Goodness, it's the whole gang." Sam smirked as

he opened the door. "What can I do for you?"

"You didn't send it, did you?" Rosie shouted. "The Tentenden Chase form… they've never received it, they say. I should never have left you to post it."

"I did post it, actually, Rosie," Sam said, calmly. "Not so many accusations, please. I'll give them a ring now and sort things out. Wait here a minute."

"Rosie, will you please calm down," Tom hissed.

A few moments later, Sam reappeared.

"It seems Rosie's right," Sam said, sounding slightly bemused. "They never received the form – it must have got lost in the post, but I can assure you I sent it. I'm sorry."

Rosie marched off towards Pepper's stable. Tom hurried after her.

"Lost in the post – what rubbish," she muttered.

"We're all disappointed," Tom said. "But I'm sure Sam wouldn't say he'd sent the form if he hadn't."

"Are you sure about that?" Rosie said. "They're useless at running Sandy Lane, so who knows what else they're capable of. I've said it before – we should let Nick and Sarah know what's going on here. School starts on Monday – Sam and Vanessa won't even have us to help them, then."

"Aren't you being a bit over-dramatic?" Tom raised his eyebrows.

"I don't think I am, Tom, no. I've not dared to say what I think for too long," Rosie said, bravely. "My mind's made up – I'm going to call them – I want to tell them what's happened. You may not care, but I wanted to enter Tentenden so much."

"We all did, Rosie," Tom snapped. His face was red and angry. "But we can't, so get over it."

Rosie pushed past Tom and strode into the tack room to get Nick and Sarah's mobile number from where they had left it, pinned to the noticeboard... But it wasn't there. She fumbled around for the scrap of paper, but there was no sign of it. A horrible thought came to her: someone didn't want anyone to talk to Nick and Sarah about what was going on at Sandy Lane. And she had a pretty good idea who that 'someone' was.

Chapter 8

Startling News

When Rosie got home, she logged straight onto her mum's laptop. *Nick and Sarah need to know what's going on*, she thought, sitting down to compose an email.

"Hi Nick and Sarah," she typed. "Please give me a call on my mobile as soon as you can. I need to speak to you very urgently – it's about Sandy Lane. Lots of love, Rosie."

As soon as she hit the send button, Rosie felt better. *At least I've tried*, she thought. She snapped the laptop shut, and went to get ready for bed.

The next thing she knew, it was half past eight the next morning. She immediately checked her mobile – no word from Nick or Sarah. *They must've seen my email by now*, Rosie thought. Then, jumping out of bed, she went downstairs to check the laptop. No messages there, either. *The internet really must be bad where they are*, she decided. Sighing, Rosie hurried back upstairs to get ready.

When Rosie finally got to the yard, everyone was standing in a group around Sam. Rosie just caught the end of what he was saying.

"...So he told me to go ahead and sell Pepper for him," Sam said.

Rosie's heart skipped a beat. She rushed up to the group. "What's going on here?" she demanded.

"Rosie, Sam spoke to Nick last night, and again this morning. Nick said that the only option was to sell Pepper," Kate said, tearfully. "He says Sandy Lane is in financial difficulty, and someone's offered a good price for him."

"That can't be right! Nick would never sell

Pepper." Rosie's face flushed pink, and tears welled up in her eyes. "He was one of their very first ponies."

"They have to. They need the money," Tom said. "I can't quite believe it myself but..."

"But Nick doesn't care about money." Rosie stared at Tom in disbelief.

"Everyone needs money, Rosie, and Sandy Lane hasn't been doing too well lately," Tom said, softly. "Plus, there are vet's bills and fodder bills to pay and all the extra expenses like their flight tickets. Blackjack's saddle alone is going to cost two weeks' earnings. Sam explained everything to him."

Nobody spoke for a few, long seconds.

"I see." Rosie sniffed and stared at the ground. "So when's Pepper going then?"

"Next Friday," Sam said, firmly.

"Next Friday?" Rosie repeated, unable to believe what she was hearing. "That's so soon."

She felt a huge lump rising in her throat. It all seemed so unreal.

"Well, we'd better get on with our work." Tom

sighed. "Try not to think about it, everyone."

Rosie nodded, but as she made her way over to Pepper's stable, she felt a wave of sadness wash over her. No more Pepper... how could that be?

She opened the little pony's stable door, and went in to stroke him. "It seems you're off next week, Pepper," she said miserably. "You'll have a new owner, but I'm sure they'll love you just as much as I do. I'm going to give you a good grooming, and let everyone see how beautiful you are."

She picked up a dandy brush used it to take the worst of the dirt off. Then, using a body brush, she worked until his whole body shone.

"Ready for our hack, Rosie?" Jess poked her head over the stable door.

"Yes, Jess." Rosie put on a brave face and smiled. "Who's taking it out?"

"Sam," Jess replied.

"Great," Rosie said, through gritted teeth. As she led Pepper across the yard, she noticed Susannah struggling with Horace's saddle. "Need any help?"

Rosie called.

"No, I can manage." Susannah smiled. "I tacked him up myself." She led him to the mounting block and scrambled on.

"Right, let's go," Sam said, impatiently.

Rosie followed on at the back as Sam led the ride out through the gate into the fields. Pepper sniffed the air excitedly.

"Are you alright, Susannah?" she called to the little girl in front.

"Fine," Susannah replied. But she didn't look it.

"Let's start with a canter," said Sam. "All meet up by the corner of that field."

Rosie looked uncertainly at Susannah. "Are you up for a canter, Susannah?"

"Sure!" she cried, circling Horace and nudging him on with her heels.

As Pepper cantered away, Rosie noticed something very odd in front of her. Susannah was sitting at an angle, and – she gasped in horror – Horace's saddle was falling off! Clinging to his mane, the little girl was slipping down his side.

"Help!" Susannah wailed.

Rosie didn't stop to think. Digging her heels into Pepper's side she pushed him forward, urging him on. The sweat rose on his neck as she pounded forward until they were neck and neck with the cantering horse. Leaning across, she grabbed Horace's reins and they swerved to the right, but it was too late. Susannah was on the ground. Sam and the others had cantered on without her.

"Are you okay?" Rosie said, jumping off Pepper.

"Yeah, I think so," Susannah said weakly, but Rosie could see that she was shaking.

"Try stretching your arms and legs. Do you hurt anywhere?" Rosie crouched down beside her.

"No, I don't think so." Susannah trembled.

Rosie breathed a sigh of relief. No broken bones, then. She took the little girl's hand and helped her to her feet.

"Are you sure you did the girth up properly?" Rosie asked, gently.

"Yes, I know I did," Susannah replied. "I double checked it too. It was really tight. I don't know how it could have come undone."

"Don't worry." Rosie smiled reassuringly – she didn't want to press her. This sort of thing could destroy a young rider's confidence. "We'll collect the saddle and you can hop back on. Then we'll go back to the yard. Here are the others."

"What's going on here?" Sam shouted, thundering over on Hector. He didn't look very sympathetic.

"The saddle came off, Sam," Rosie called. "Susannah fell off."

"Stupid girl!" Sam shouted, turning to Susannah. "You can't have done the girth up properly."

"I'm sorry, Sam," Susannah whimpered. "I was sure I had."

Rosie was furious. A telling off was the last thing Susannah needed.

"Come on Susannah." Rosie shot Sam a dirty look. "I'll go back to the stables with you."

"Did you have to do that?" she said to Sam, as

Susannah turned away. "She was really shaken."

"She has to learn, Rosie, and I'll thank you not to talk to me like that," Sam growled. "Take her back to the yard and I'll speak to you later."

Jess, who had just caught the end of the conversation, looked confused. "Rosie, are you happy to go back with Susannah?" she asked.

"I'll be fine," said Rosie. "You go ahead. The ride's been ruined for me anyway."

Jess smiled apologetically, and turned to catch up with the others.

"Don't take any notice of that horrible man, Susannah," Rosie said. "When I had just started learning to ride, I put the saddle on the wrong way round!" This wasn't technically true, but at least it brought a smile to Susannah's face. "Can you get the saddle while I hold onto Horace and Pepper?"

As Susannah ran over to pick up the saddle, the little girl gasped. "Rosie, look!" she cried, holding out the saddle for Rosie to see. "I knew I'd done it up properly. See what's under the saddle flap."

Rosie looked: the girth had snapped in two.

"It must have been rotten," Susannah said. "That's so dangerous."

"You're right," Rosie peered at the saddle. "Well, we can't ride back to the yard now, if that's the case. If you can hold the saddle in place on Horace's back, I'll lead the horses."

As the two girls walked back together, they chatted away as normal. Susannah seemed to have recovered from her fall and her telling-off from Sam.

"Could you groom Horace?" Rosie asked, when they arrived back at the stable.

"Of course." Susannah nodded eagerly.

Rosie smiled. She was a tough cookie, this girl. "You lead these two back to their stables," she suggested. "I'll take the saddle."

Taking the saddle, Rosie hurried into the tack room, where she examined the girth closely. Girths didn't just snap in two, she knew: it had been cut. It must have been hanging by a thread when Susannah tacked up. But who could have done such a dangerous, foolish thing?

She needed time to think. There was something niggling her, something that held the key to it all. But what was it?

Suddenly, she knew what it was. Rosie stopped in her tracks. Why hadn't any of them thought of it before? She had to speak to Beth.

"Hey, what are you doing heading off so early?" Alex called out, as Rosie crossed the yard.

"Susannah took a tumble. Could you sort her out, please?" Rosie grabbed the handlebars of her bike.

"Okay, but where are you going?"

"Tell you when I get back," Rosie said, jumping on her bike. "Just tell Sam that I've gone home for lunch or something."

"But..." Alex started.

"See you in a bit!" she called back, as she sped off down the drive. She didn't want to waste one more second. This needed to be done, and fast.

Chapter 9

A Chilling Discovery

Rosie felt nervous as she got near Beth's house. She wanted to explain exactly what had been going on, and not let it all spill out in a gabbled, angry rush.

"Double bookings, reduced takings, Whisp's lameness, the missing saddle, the Tentenden entry form, the phonecall about Pepper, the sabotaged girth," she said aloud to herself. There was only one thing she couldn't explain – the reason why all these things were happening.

Beth would know what to do, she was sure. She

rang the doorbell, and waited until Mrs. Wilson opened the door.

"Hello, Mrs. Wilson. Is Beth in please?"

"Oh Rosie, great to see you. Come on in." Mrs. Wilson ushered her inside.

"How is she?" Rosie asked.

"Oh, much better. Another few weeks and she'll be back with you." Mrs. Wilson took her into the living room, where Beth was sitting on the sofa.

"Rosie!" Beth cried. "I've been hoping you'd come round. Thank you so much for looking after me after the accident. I don't know what would have happened if you hadn't been there."

Rosie smiled. "Don't mention it," she said, bashfully. She felt a bit embarrassed – she hadn't even come to ask about Beth's leg.

"So, tell me your news. How are things at the stables? Mum told me there were some new people helping out," Beth went on, cheerfully.

"That's sort of what I've come to talk to you about," Rosie said. "It's not good. I need your help."

"Why, what is it?" Beth asked, concerned.

"I'm not sure." Rosie took a deep breath. "I think I'd better start at the beginning."

Beth propped herself up as Rosie started to go through everything that had happened. She tried to explain it all clearly, until she got to that morning, and the news about Pepper.

"Apparently Sam spoke to Nick on the phone. Nick's asked him to sell Pepper," Rosie recounted. "But it can't be right. That would be the last thing Nick and Sarah would do if they were in financial trouble, not the first."

"I agree." Beth shook her head. "It's a crazy idea."

"I know, and that's when I started thinking..." Rosie lowered her voice. "I don't think Sam has been speaking to Nick at all."

"What do you mean?" Beth asked.

Rosie stopped to draw breath. She knew what she was about to say sounded silly and far-fetched.

"I think Sam might have made the whole thing up," Rosie blurted out. "I don't think they would ever sell Pepper, however bad things were."

Beth's face was grave. "I think I'd better come to the stables with you and find out what's going on." She reached for her crutches. "I'll see if Mum will drive us there. Where did Sam and Vanessa come from anyway? What did Nick tell you about them? And whatever happened to Dick Bryant, the man Nick wanted you to ask for help if you needed it? There are so many unanswered questions..."

"We haven't spoken to Nick since he left – his number's gone missing from the notice board," Rosie explained. "I emailed him last night, but they don't have a very good internet connection where they are. You're the only one who has spoken to him."

"But I haven't spoken to him." Beth stared at Rosie in alarm.

"Yes, you have," Rosie replied. "When you called him and told him about your accident."

"I didn't phone him," Beth insisted.

"Well we didn't either..." Rosie's face went pale. *If none of them had phoned Nick and Sarah, who had?*

Unless... unless Sam and Vanessa hadn't been sent by Nick and Sarah at all.

Rosie felt a shiver run up her spine. "Come on, let's go," she whispered.

A short drive later, and the two girls were back at the bottom of Sandy Lane. Waving goodbye to Mrs. Wilson, Beth and Rosie decided on a plan of action.

"I'd better arrive after you, Rosie," Beth said, leaning against her crutches. "I've got to appear just to be calling in on the off chance."

"Good thinking," said Rosie. "And we must phone Nick and Sarah as soon as we can."

"But how can we get hold of them?" said Beth. "You said the number had gone."

"You must have it though, haven't you?" Rosie said pleadingly.

"No I don't." Beth shook her head guiltily. "I didn't think I'd need it if we had it in the tack room."

"What are we going to do?" Rosie replied. "We can't ask Sam and Vanessa for the number. Even if they've got it, they'll never give it to us. They're trying to stop us telling Nick what they're doing. Should we go to the police?"

"First, I think we need to find out exactly what they're doing, and why," said Beth. "Nobody will believe us if we don't do that."

"You're right," Rosie said, setting off up the drive. "You wait here until I've gone up."

Beth nodded, and after waiting for a few minutes, she hobbled up the drive and into the yard. There, she was immediately surrounded by excited faces and lots of questions.

"Beth, how's your leg?"

"Have you missed us?"

"Are you back for good?"

Beth smiled wearily. "I'd be a bit useless with this thing, wouldn't I?" She pointed to her plaster cast. "I've just come to see how you're getting on."

"Not great." Kate looked gloomy. "The takings have been down all week."

"Where are Sam and Vanessa?" Rosie asked.

"Gone out again," Tom replied. "There was a

telephone call. They had to rush off… said they'd be back in an hour."

"Good timing." Rosie's face relaxed.

"What do you mean?" Jess looked at her friend.

"Listen guys, Rosie and I have got something to tell you about our friends Sam and Vanessa," Beth announced. "I think we'd better go somewhere more private. Just in case they come back."

"I don't know where to begin," Rosie said, as everybody huddled into the tack room.

"Start at the beginning… as you did with me," Beth said encouragingly.

"Okay." Rosie took a deep breath and began the story at the very beginning… starting with her doubts about Sam and Vanessa, right through to the phone calls to Nick that she was convinced had never happened.

Then, when Rosie explained that Beth hadn't called Nick and Sarah at all, everyone gasped.

"So where have Sam and Vanessa come from?" Kate cried.

"'That's what we need to find out," Beth said.

"I just can't believe it..." Tom sounded crestfallen. "And I've been defending Sam this whole time. I'm sorry Rosie. I should have listened to you."

Rosie sighed. "I know you were just trying to do the right thing, Tom. But we need to fix this situation as soon as possible. Sam and Vanessa can't be allowed to get away with it."

"I think we should phone Nick and Sarah right away." Tom reached for the phone.

Rosie and Beth exchanged nervous glances.

"We can't, Tom," said Rosie. "Nobody has Nick's contact number. I looked for it last night, and it's gone from the notice board."

"What?" Tom glanced at the notice board in panic. "Well, we could email them then?"

Rosie shook her head. "I've already tried. They're not picking any emails up."

"We should go to the police," Kate suggested.

"And say what?" Rosie sighed.

"Rosie and I have a plan, so listen up," Beth

interrupted. "We don't want Sam and Vanessa suspecting something's up, and we certainly can't accuse them of anything until we're sure what's going on. We have to behave as normally as possible for a few days while we check them out."

"But we go back to school on Monday," Tom reminded her. "Who'll look after the yard? Nick and Sarah aren't back until Saturday."

"If you introduce me to them, I'll offer to help out while you're all at school," Beth replied. "I know I won't be much good around the yard, but they'll need someone to take bookings. I can keep an eye on things, and it sounds as if they need the help."

"You're right there." Tom frowned.

"Great. So all agreed?" Beth looked at the group.

"But what about Pepper?" Rosie asked. "He's supposed to be sold on Friday. If we don't put a stop to Sam and Vanessa soon, he'll be gone."

"Well, we'll just have to take him ourselves and hide him somewhere," Beth said.

"What? Where?" Rosie was shocked – this was

getting serious.

"There's Mr. Green's pig farm," Tom suggested. "It's near enough to the stables, but no one would think to look in one of the outbuildings at the back."

"But what if Sam and Vanessa report Pepper as stolen?" Kate asked.

"I may be wrong, but I think they'll want to avoid the police getting involved at all costs," Beth said. "Right, I can hear a car coming, so act normal and get on with your jobs."

It was Sam's car, pulling into the yard. He climbed out and walked over to the group, as they emptied out of the tack room.

"Hi Sam," Tom called, smiling awkwardly. "Come and meet Beth, our stable girl."

Rosie watched Sam's face closely as he leant over to shake Beth's hand. He looked surprised, but covered it up quickly.

"Pleased to meet you. I heard about your accident. How's the leg?" Sam asked.

"Oh, n-n-not too bad," Beth stuttered.

Rosie noticed that the colour had suddenly drained from Beth's face. What was going on? Sam was bound to guess something was wrong by just looking at her! Rosie gave her a sharp nudge.

"C-can I help with the bookings?" Beth continued, avoiding Sam's eyes.

"That's kind of you," said Sam. "We'll be rushed off our feet when the regulars are back at school."

"Well, I am getting pretty bored at home to be honest." Beth smiled weakly.

"That's settled then," said Sam. "Now, what have we got on this afternoon?"

"You're giving a lesson at three," Tom replied. "I'll make a start on getting the horses tacked up."

"I'll get a cup of tea at the cottage and then I'll join you." Sam nodded.

"I'll help you with Pepper, Rosie." Beth forced a frozen smile in Sam's direction, as he walked away.

"You don't have to," Rosie said. "Why don't you sit down and rest your leg? You look tired."

"No, I'd like to help," Beth said forcefully,

following her over to Pepper's stable.

Rosie drew back the bolt and let them inside. Beth closed the door behind her and leaned against the wall. She was still very pale.

"What is it Beth? You look as if you've seen a ghost," Rosie said. "You almost gave the game away back there. Are you sure you're going to be all right here on your own next week?"

"Yes, I'm fine. It's not that, Rosie. I've just had a terrible shock. You see, I recognize Sam."

Rosie frowned. "Where from?"

Beth took a deep breath. "If I'm not mistaken, Sam was the driver of that car... The one that almost ran me down."

"What!" Rosie gasped. "The red sports car? Are you sure?"

"Quite sure," said Beth. "Sam was definitely the man that could have killed me, Rosie."

Chapter 10

Midnight Ride

Rosie stared at Beth in horror. What other terrible things could Sam Durant be capable of, if he could almost run someone down and drive away? Everything was starting to fall into place: Sam and Vanessa somehow knowing about the accident, and their arriving so promptly after it had happened. It all added up. Suddenly, Sam's face appeared at the stable door.

"Everything alright in here?" he said, his beady eyes fixed on them both.

Rosie jumped back. "Yes, f-f-f-fine." How long

had he been listening outside? Was he aware of their suspicions? Beth froze as Sam walked away.

"Beth, I'm sure he knows something. We've got to get Pepper out of here fast," Rosie whispered.

"We'll have to be careful," Beth breathed. "If we take him too soon, we won't find out what they're up to and the police won't believe us."

"What if you told them that Sam was driving that car?" Rosie felt desperate.

"But I said in my statement that I couldn't remember what the man looked like, and I wasn't lying. Seeing him today jogged my memory, but it probably wouldn't convict him in court. We have to get some hard evidence. It's probably best if you or one of the others take Pepper on Thursday evening."

Rosie gulped. "That late? Someone's coming to collect him on Friday."

"No," said Beth firmly. "That's the best plan. I'll be here, on the look out, and I'll let you know of any developments."

The next few days passed painfully slowly for

Rosie. She found it almost impossible to concentrate in school, but Beth reported that nothing much was happening at the yard. She thought Sam and Vanessa must be planning something big before Nick and Sarah returned – but when would they strike?

Beth phoned her on Thursday evening. "So who's going to take Pepper to Mr. Green's pig farm?"

"I am." Rosie gulped. "Tom and Jess both offered, but I think it's best if just one of us goes. We're less likely to get caught that way. I've set my alarm for eleven thirty."

"And you know exactly where you're taking Pepper, don't you?"

"The old shed by the huge barn."

"Yep. Good luck!"

Rosie put down the phone and looked at her watch. Nine o'clock... Eleven thirty seemed like an eternity away. She went downstairs and poked her head around the door of the sitting room.

"Mum, I'm shattered." Rosie exaggerated a yawn. "I think I'll get an early night."

"Okay, love," Rosie's mother glanced up from her book. "Sleep well."

In her room, Rosie double-checked that she had everything: torch, pony nuts and riding hat. Her heart was pounding. Finally, her watch said twenty past eleven, and it was time to go. Pulling on her jodhpurs and an extra layer, she crept downstairs and out through the front door.

All was quiet on the street – not a soul was around. The trees cast spooky silhouettes all around her, so she pedalled as hard as she could to get to Sandy Lane.

When she rolled into the yard, all the lights were on in the cottage. What were Sam and Vanessa doing, up so late? Leaving her bike hidden underneath a bush, she ducked down and stole up to the cottage, where she hid under the sitting room window. She recognised Vanessa's voice first.

"You're taking things too far now, Ralph."

Rosie froze. Who on earth was 'Ralph'?

"I haven't gone far enough," Sam said. "Messing

up the bookings and sabotaging saddles is not going to ruin Sandy Lane's reputation fast enough. Nick Brooks is back on Saturday. I've got to destroy Sandy Lane, once and for all."

Rosie staggered back into the bush behind her, knocking over a dustbin as she did.

"Who's there?" Sam opened the front door.

Rosie held her breath, desperately hoping that the bush would hide her.

"There's no one there, Ralph," Vanessa said, peering out behind him. "Come to bed – it's a busy day tomorrow. Pepper's being collected isn't he? What have you done about payment for him?"

"Cash on delivery, that was the deal." Sam retreated back inside. "Right, let's get some sleep."

Rosie waited as Sam closed the door, trying to absorb what she had just heard. Finally, the lights went off in the cottage and she headed back over to Pepper's stable.

"Sshh boy. We've got to get you away from here," she said, stepping inside his stable with a handful of pony nuts. Beth had left all the tack out ready for her, as she'd promised to. But there was no time for a saddle: she'd have to ride bareback.

Leading Pepper out of the stable, Rosie turned him towards the fields that led to Mr. Green's pig farm. Then, with a quick backwards glance, she vaulted onto the little pony's back and they were off, into the darkness together.

All was quiet as they walked out of the woods and crossed the road. This was the bit where they had to be careful. If Sam – or whoever he really was – had heard them leave, he would be bound to come searching for them by car. But there was no sound at all. Taking the back route into Mr. Green's pig farm, Rosie headed straight for the shed.

"No one will think to look for you here, Pepper," she whispered, jumping to the ground. "I know it's not what you're used to, but you'll be safe."

She took off his bridle and shut the little pony in the shed. "I'm going to have to leave you now – before anyone notices I'm missing." She patted

Pepper fondly. "Don't worry, Jess will bring your breakfast in the morning."

Pepper snickered as Rosie filled the trough with water. She wished she could stay with him all night, but she had to be up early. They needed to make plans, if that fraud of a man and his horrible wife were hatching a scheme to destroy Sandy Lane. Whatever it took, they had to be stopped.

Chapter 11

Plans

"Sam's been running around cursing, accusing everyone imaginable of stealing Pepper," Beth said, when she rang Rosie at home the next day. "You're top on his list of suspects by the way, but he won't call the police, just as I suspected. He..."

"Beth, listen!" Rosie interrupted. "I overheard Sam and Vanessa talking at the cottage last night... The double bookings, the cancelled rides... They did it all on purpose, to ruin Sandy Lane's reputation."

The line went quiet for a moment before Beth spoke. "Why would they want to do such a terrible thing? It doesn't make any sense," she said, quietly.

"I don't know why, but they're certainly no friends of Nick and Sarah's. They're planning to do something so serious it will destroy Sandy Lane before they get back."

"Are you sure you heard things right?" Beth said.

"Yes! We've got to go to the police, Beth. This is getting out of control," Rosie cried.

"But what do we tell them?" Beth replied. "That you overheard a conversation at the cottage in the middle of the night? We need proof of exactly what Sam and Vanessa are up to. Look, Nick and Sarah are due back tomorrow, aren't they?"

"Yes," Rosie said slowly.

"Then we'll just have to sit tight and keep watch." Beth took a deep breath. "Whatever Sam and Vanessa have got planned, they've got to make their move soon. If we can get firm evidence of wrongdoing, we can go to the police. Listen, you go to school and I'll think of a plan. Do you think you can get everyone to meet me at eight this evening at the bottom of the drive?"

"Yes," said Rosie. "I'll text everyone."

"Good." Beth's voice sounded calmer now.

"But Beth," Rosie said uncertainly. "What if we can't stop them?"

"We will, Rosie," Beth answered. "We have to."

It was dusk when everyone met up at the bottom of the drive. They were all horrified after Rosie had told them what she had overheard.

"Okay," Beth started. "We've got to decide on a plan of action. We don't know exactly what Sam and Vanessa are going to do, but whatever it is, we've got to catch them red-handed, which means watching them twenty-four seven from now on."

"But what do we tell our parents?" Rosie asked, looking worried.

"I don't think we should tell anyone anything yet," Beth replied. "We'll use the tack room, the barn, the cottage, the outdoor school and three of the stables as lookout points. At the first sign of trouble, we call the police, but let's try not to raise the alarm until we know what they're up to and can prove it."

Everybody nodded in acceptance.

"Right, everyone into position," Beth finished, nodding at the group.

Rosie crept to the back of the stables, and glimpsed Sam and Vanessa moving around in the cottage. Their Range Rover boot was wide open and she could see Nick's silver racing trophies piled up inside it. She tiptoed closer, pausing near the window so she could hear their conversation.

"We can't wait for Pepper to show up any longer," Sam said. "I'm sure those kids have taken him somewhere. We really needed that money..."

"It's more important that we clear out of here quickly, with whatever we can grab," Vanessa urged. "They're onto us – it's time to go."

As much as she would have liked to have stayed and listened, Rosie dragged herself along to the big barn. Climbing on top of the haybales, Rosie settled down to wait. Within minutes, she could feel herself drifting off – she was so tired after her broken night moving Pepper. One thing kept rising to the surface of her mind: who was this man 'Ralph'? The name was so familiar, somehow...

She was woken by shouting, and a strange, strong smell in the yard. It reminded her of a garage... Then she realized – it was petrol!

Peering over the top of the hay bales, she saw Sam and Vanessa carrying large cans across the yard. Rosie started to panic as she scrambled out of the hay. Fire! They had meant exactly what they had said. They were going to destroy Sandy Lane once and for all – they were planning to burn Sandy Lane down! Before she had time to do anything at all, she saw Tom step out from the shadows and shout across the yard.

"Just stop right there." Tom's voice echoed around the stables.

Sam seemed startled for a moment, then he saw who it was and started to laugh. He put down the petrol can he was carrying, and pulled a cigarette lighter from his pocket.

"So you're going to stop me, are you, Tom?" Sam jeered, flicking the lighter in his hand.

Rosie held her breath. If Tom didn't act quickly, Sandy Lane would go up in flames. She had to do something... She scrambled down from the haybales and into the yard.

"We know what your game is," Rosie shouted. Her heart thumped inside her chest as she walked towards Sam. "I think the police will be very interested in what we have to say."

Sam laughed. "By the time you've told your little tales, Sandy Lane will be history."

"You may be out of here, but we'll know where to find you, Ralph... Ralph Winterson," Rosie said, feeling a burst of bravery.

Sam looked startled.

"Isn't that your real name?" Rosie went on. "You're Ralph Winterson, owner of the Clarendon Equestrian Centre, aren't you? Been exposed for cruelty to horses, haven't you?"

Tom gasped. For a moment there was silence. Then the stillness of the yard was broken by the sound of clapping.

"You've certainly done your homework, Rosie," Ralph challenged. Sneering, he clapped his hands together in mock applause. "But you can't prove a word of it, nobody ever could."

"I can, actually," Rosie said calmly. "I have evidence to prove it – I recorded a conversation between you and Vanessa on my phone last night, as you chatted about double bookings and cancelled rides. Ring any bells?"

"You're bluffing," Ralph replied. But from the look on his face, Rosie knew that he wasn't sure.

"It's all saved on my phone at home," Rosie went on. "Did you really think you could ruin Sandy Lane's reputation so easily, or that you could drive anyone to come to your lousy stables instead?"

"So are you going to hand the recording over to the police, then?" Ralph growled.

"Well, I could..." Rosie paused, looking at Ralph steadily. "But I won't."

The others gasped. Tom seemed as if he was about to say something, but Rosie held up her hand to silence him.

"You won't?" Ralph replied.

"I won't do anything with the recording, on one condition..." Rosie said slowly. "I want you to close down the Clarendon Equestrian Centre immediately, pack your bags and disappear out of this neighbourhood for good."

Ralph opened his mouth to speak, but he knew he was beaten. He put the lighter back in his pocket, jutted out his chin, and turned to go.

"And one more thing," Rosie called sharply. "You can put Nick's racing trophies back where you found them, too."

Ralph shot her an angry glance. "Come on, Vanessa." He beckoned to his wife, who dropped the petrol can she had been carrying on the ground. "We've got better things to do."

Everything had happened so quickly. One minute, Ralph held the future of Sandy Lane in his hand, the next, he and Vanessa had shut up the boot of their Range Rover and were speeding out of the yard.

"Let's hope that's the last we see of them," Rosie muttered, as the Range Rover screeched down the drive and disappeared.

"Rosie, you were amazing," Jess cried, rushing over to hug her friend. "I can't believe you worked all that out for yourself."

"Just a bit of detective work. No big deal." Rosie smiled bashfully.

"But to record their conversation as proof, that's incredible." Tom shook his head in admiration.

"Actually, I didn't." Rosie laughed. "That was just a bluff. But it did the job, didn't it?"

Chapter 12

Nick and Sarah Return

The regulars spent all the next morning getting rid of the petrol-soaked straw and clearing up the stables, ready for Nick and Sarah's return. Rosie had brought Pepper back home and settled him in with the other horses.

"So that explains the 'For Sale' board outside the Clarendon Equestrian Centre," said Susannah, as Rosie finished retelling the story. "Everyone's been talking about it."

Rosie smiled thoughtfully.

"But there's one thing I don't understand,"

Susannah went on. "Why didn't you go straight to the police when you found out what Ralph and Vanessa were up to?"

"Well..." Rosie hesitated. "Firstly we didn't really know what they were doing until the very last minute, and secondly, we didn't have any evidence. It would have been my word against theirs."

"I guess you're right." Susannah nodded.

Rosie looked around the yard. "Okay, is everyone here now?" She smiled as the regulars all gathered around. "Listen up. I've just had some exciting news... We'll be riding in the Tentenden Team Chase next weekend after all! I phoned them this morning, just in time it appears."

Everyone gasped.

Rosie grinned mischievously. "And guess what... It seems one of the teams has dropped out."

"Which one?" Tom asked.

"The Clarendon Equestrian Centre!" Rosie's eyes sparkled. "So we can take their place."

"What?" Tom shrieked.

"That's brilliant!" Jess whooped, throwing her riding hat in the air.

Rosie beamed as she looked around at the delighted faces of her friends. In her dreams, the Tentenden trophy had long been theirs. Now they actually had the chance to win it!

At that moment, a car rounded the corner and pulled up in the yard. Then there were voices – voices they all recognized. Nick and Sarah had returned from America! Ebony went wild and launched himself upon them as they stepped out of the taxi.

"Woah boy, now calm down," Nick laughed, patting Ebony gently. "Hi everyone." He grinned as everyone gathered around the taxi. "Phew. It's great to be home. I don't suppose much has happened here, but we've got some amazing stories to tell you about America."

Rosie smiled, and looked at the others. "We've got some pretty amazing stories to tell you, too!"